First published 1992 by Walker Books Ltd
87 Vauxhall Walk, London SE11 5HJ

This edition published 2018

2 4 6 8 10 9 7 5 3 1

Text © 1992 Jon Blake
Illustrations © 1992 Axel Scheffler

The right of Jon Blake and Axel Scheffler to be identified
as author and illustrator respectively of this work
has been asserted by them in accordance with
the Copyright, Designs and Patents Act 1988

This book has been typeset in Veronan

Printed in China

British Library Cataloguing in Publication Data:
a catalogue record for this book is available from the British Library

ISBN 978-1-4063-8565-6

www.walker.co.uk

You're a Hero, Daley B!

Jon Blake   illustrated by Axel Scheffler

WALKER BOOKS
AND SUBSIDIARIES
LONDON · BOSTON · SYDNEY · AUCKLAND

Daley B didn't
know what
he was.

"Am I a monkey?" he said.
"Am I a koala?"
"Am I a porcupine?"

Daley B didn't know where to live.

"Should I live
in a cave?"
he said.

"Should I live in a nest?"

"Should I live in a web?"

Daley B didn't know what to eat.

"Should I
eat fish?"
he said.

"Should I eat potatoes?"

"Should I eat worms?"

Daley B didn't know why his feet were so big.

"Are they for water-skiing?" he said.

"Are they for the mice to sit on?"

"Are they to keep the rain off?"

Daley B saw the birds in the tree, and decided he would live in a tree.

Daley B saw the squirrels eating acorns,
and decided he would eat acorns.

But he still didn't know why his feet were so big.

One day, there was great panic in the
woodland. All the rabbits gathered
beneath Daley B's tree.
"You must come down at
once, Daley B!" they cried.
"Jazzy D is coming!"
"Who is Jazzy D?" asked Daley B.
The rabbits were too excited to answer.
They scattered across the grass and
vanished into their burrows.

Daley B stayed in his tree, and nibbled another acorn, and wondered about his big feet.

Jazzy D crept out of the bushes.
Her teeth were as sharp as broken glass,
and her eyes were as quick as fleas.

Jazzy D sneaked around the burrows, but
there was not a rabbit to be seen.

Jazzy D looked up.
Daley B waved.

Jazzy D began to climb the tree.
The other rabbits poked out their
noses, and trembled.

"Hello," said Daley B to Jazzy D.

"Are you a badger?"

"Are you an elephant?"

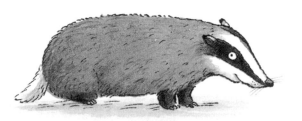

"Are you a duck-billed platypus?"

Jazzy D crept closer. "No, my friend,"
she whispered, "I am a weasel."

"Do you live in a pond?" asked Daley B.

"Do you live in a dam?"

"Do you live in a kennel?"

Jazzy D crept closer still.
"No, my friend," she hissed, "I live
in the darkest corner of the wood."

"Do you eat cabbages?" asked Daley B.

"Do you eat insects?"

"Do you eat fruit?"

Jazzy D crept right up to Daley B.
"No, my friend," she rasped,
"I eat rabbits! Rabbits like *you*!"

Daley B's face fell.
"Am I ... a rabbit?" he stammered.

Jazzy D nodded ... and licked her lips ...

and leapt!

Daley B didn't have to think. Quick as a flash,
he turned his back, and kicked out with his massive feet.
Jazzy D sailed through the air, far far away,
back where she came from.

The other rabbits jumped and cheered
and hugged each other.
"You're a hero, Daley B!" they cried.

"That's funny," said Daley B.
"I thought I was
a rabbit."

Jon Blake is the author of over fifty books for children, teenagers and adults. His work is noted for its originality and humour; successes include *Little Stupendo*, *One Girl School* and the *House of Fun* series. Jon was brought up in Southampton and now lives in Cardiff.

Axel Scheffler is an award-winning illustrator who has achieved worldwide acclaim for his warm and colourful illustrations, and has created many bestselling children's books including *The Gruffalo*, written by Julia Donaldson. Born in Hamburg, Axel studied at Bath Academy of Art and worked in advertising, magazines and newspapers before turning to children's books. *You're a Hero, Daley B!* was his first picture book ever. Axel now lives in London.